Beast Quest®

MAKORO
THE BLINDING
STINGER

BY ADAM BLADE

ORCHARD

THE NEW PROTECTORS!

NOLAN

KATYA

RAFE

MIANDRA

Welcome to the world of Beast Quest!

When a series of Beast attacks shocked the peaceful land of Tangala, Queen Aroha called for a worthy Master or Mistress of the Beasts. But one fighter wasn't enough for the grave danger the kingdom faced, and four candidates pledged their weapons to the Queen to restore peace. There is strength in unity and power in friendship. Together, Katya from the Forest of Shadows, Nolan of Aran, Miandra from the western shore and Rafe of Doran will venture to new lands and battle enemies of the realm. The fate of Tangala is in their hands.

While there's blood in their veins, the New Protectors will never give up the Quest...

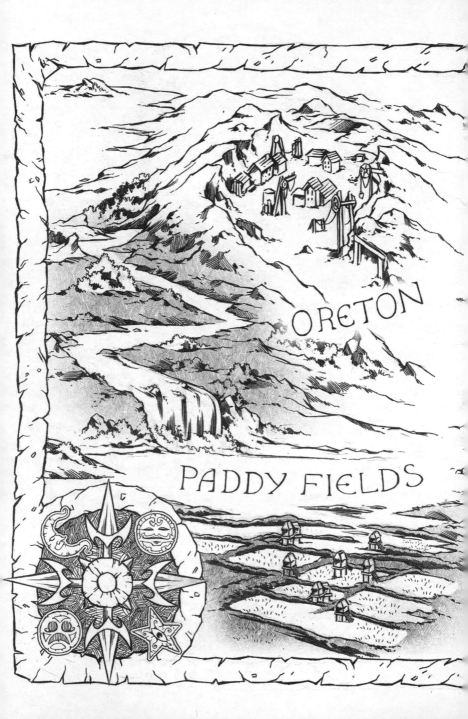

ORETON

PADDY FIELDS

There are special gold coins to collect in this book. You will earn one coin for every chapter you read.

Find out what to do with your coins at the end of the book.

CONTENTS

A new band of so-called "heroes" have gathered, trained by Tom of Avantia, to keep Tangala safe and serve Queen Aroha. Ha! My family ruled these lands long before there was any talk of kings and queens. Before even the name "Tangala" was coined.

We were the Metamorphia – the sorcerers of change – who learned our magic in the depths of the Netherworld. We shaped the essence of creation. Beasts were slaves to our will.

Alas, the rulers of Tangala attempted to consign us to history and now I am the last of my line. But I will not fade into memory or myth. I will show our New Protectors who really rules this kingdom. Their weapons will be useless, and their courage will fail them when they encounter my creations.

Zuba

RATS IN A TRAP

CLANG!

The sound echoed through the shadowy corridor as the prison door swung shut. There was a clunk as a muscular guard turned a key in the lock. Tom could see Hyrold through the bars, slumped against the wall of the cell. The hulking bandit looked up. His two remaining teeth glinted in the dim torchlight.

Even prison must be better than what he's just been through, thought

Tom, with a shudder. He could still feel the bruises from his fight with Hyrix, the terrifying human-goat hybrid that Hyrold had been magically transformed into until Tom had prevailed.

"I hope you find some peace," said Tom quietly, before he turned away and followed the guard up a spiral staircase to the upper floors of the palace. Queen Aroha's fortress was built out of sandy red stone, like the rest of the city of Pania, and the walls of the corridors were hung with the banners of Tangala, her kingdom.

Tom winced with every step. He

hadn't recovered from Malvel's foul poison, let alone the effort of defeating Hyrix.

Still...at least I've got company on this Quest.

Waiting outside the great bronze doors of the Queen's throne room was Elenna, Tom's best friend, and Rafe, one of Tangala's four New Protectors. Rafe was no older than Tom had been when he set out on his very first Beast Quest, and he was every bit as brave. It made Tom smile to see the look of determination in the boy's serious blue eyes. It gave him hope for the future.

"The Queen didn't mess around, did she?" said Elenna. "She must have had builders working overtime to rebuild the dungeon."

"Just as well," said Tom. "We'll need to fill those prison cells."

Hyrold had been safely recaptured, but the rest of his gang were still out there, scattered across Tangala. Lenka. Selma. Mackey. The wicked sorceress Zuba had set them all free. But she had cursed them so that they would each transform into a hideous Beast.

Now, only the New Protectors of Tangala had a hope of tracking down the bandits and bringing them to justice. *With a little help from me and Elenna, of course.*

Elenna grinned, pushing open the doors of the throne room and bowing low. "After you, Master of the Beasts."

Tom smiled and stepped into a cavernous hall with a high, arched ceiling. Shafts of sunlight speared through tall windows, making the white marble floor gleam. But his spirits fell when he saw that the silver throne at the end of the hall was empty.

"Where's Queen Aroha?" he asked a servant who was high up on a ladder, dusting behind a tapestry.

"She's meeting with an ambassador from Gwildor," came the reply.

"I suppose a queen's work is never done," said Elenna, with a sly smile.

"A servant's work is never done, more like," said the man as he came down the ladder. "Scram!" He stamped his foot at a scrawny black cat, which darted round behind the throne.

A familiar figure came bustling in through a side door. Tom's heart lifted to see his old friend Daltec, dressed in his wizard's robes.

"Such a relief to see you again," said

Daltec. "Each Quest seems more perilous than the last."

"I only hope this latest one is really over," muttered Elenna, casting a glance at Rafe.

"You can show him now," Tom told the boy.

Rafe stepped forward, still looking a little awed to be in the presence of such a powerful wizard. He held out the hammer he had used on his Quest. "Something happened to it when we defeated Hyrix," said Rafe, frowning. "This strange purple smoke spilled out of the Beast's body... It seemed to flow into my

hammer. Then it disappeared."

Daltec peered at the hammer, one eyebrow raised. "It doesn't look any different."

Rafe shook his head. "It doesn't feel any different either. I was thinking the smoke might be... magical?"

"Oh, undoubtedly," said Daltec. "But I've never heard of such a thing before. I shall have to consult the palace library. Until then, perhaps it's best if I look after this." He carefully took the hammer from Rafe's hands. "As for you, Tom..." He gave Tom a stern look. "You need rest if you are to recover."

Tom opened his mouth to protest, but the wizard carried on regardless. "The New Protectors

will call on you if you are needed."
Daltec nodded at the golden ring on
Tom's finger, its red gemstone softly
glowing. Tom knew that every one
of the young heroes wore a similar
ring, each with a magical gemstone
that Daltec had crafted.

He's right, Tom told himself. *They'll
tell me if they need me.* He felt his
muscles relax at the thought of rest.
"I suppose we're all safe enough
here in the palace," he admitted.

Outside, the sky seemed to
darken, throwing them all into
shadow. A chill spread through the
throne room, the banners on the

walls rippling as though stirred by a breeze that Tom couldn't feel.

BANG! A sudden gust of wind slammed a door shut, making them all jump.

"What the...?" muttered Elenna.

Then a high, cruel laugh rang out. An echoey laugh that set Tom's spine tingling. His hand flew to his sword hilt.

The little black cat hopped up on to the empty throne. Tom gasped as he saw its fur shrink into its body, which pulsed and swelled until it had transformed into something else entirely.

Now, a young woman sprawled carelessly on the throne with one leg across the arm rest. Her long hair was as black as a raven's feathers, and her eyes were blacker still. She wore a silver gown, and in one hand she held a staff of knotty, darkened Wyrwood, forked at one end like a dragon's horns.

Zuba!

Tom started forwards, ready to draw his sword, but the sorceress only laughed again. "So you haven't learned your lesson yet," she sneered. "You cannot save this kingdom. You are as pitiful and

helpless as rats caught in a trap —
no matter how much you squirm,
Tangala will fall!"

"We'll see about that," snarled
Elenna. Tom saw that she already

had an arrow fitted to her bow. She let fly, just as Zuba let out another horrible cackle.

Whhssshhh-thunk!

The arrow buried itself in the back of the throne, quivering slightly.

But the wicked sorceress was already gone. She had melted into the air, leaving behind only a plume of black smoke that drifted lazily up towards the beams.

Sunlight streamed in through the windows once again. But the chill inside the throne room lingered.

CRAFTY MACKEY

"Faster, you wretch!"

Mackey jerked at the reins, but the horse couldn't muster more than a feeble half-trot. It stumbled on the scree and slowed again to a weary trudge.

It was all too much – the long journey, the endless rocks and the cruel heat of the beating sun. Mackey swiped sweat from his brow. He felt terrible. *Is it just the heat?* he wondered. *Or is it that witch's potion?*

Mackey wasn't sure what she'd done to him, but he knew he hadn't felt right since he'd drunk the concoction and fled Pania. Now he barely knew where he was — the ground was uneven, the terrain dusty and red and featureless as far as he could see. His head was spinning, and he thought he might be sick.

Suddenly he slipped from his

saddle and tumbled to the rocky ground. "Yargh!" His shoulder jarred against a rock. He curled up in pain.

With a whinny, the horse put on a sudden burst of speed and galloped

clumsily away. In a moment it had disappeared behind a rocky outcrop.

Mackey cursed and spat. *I knew that ungrateful nag was holding back on me!*

He rose unsteadily. It wasn't just the sun, he realised – the ground was hot too. "Volcanoes near here..." he muttered. "I remember now."

His skin prickled at the danger. But at the same time he felt something else – a strange sense of belonging. *This is where I'm supposed to be.* The thought made no sense, and he shrugged it off.

He carried on, his legs aching
with every step. Without the horse
he was slower still. His throat was
dry. What he wouldn't give for a sip
of water...

"Whoa!" He lurched to a halt,
heart pounding. Up ahead, the
ground came to a sudden end.
Beyond, there was nothing – just
a sheer drop, the bottom so far
below it made his stomach churn. A
canyon.

He began to back away, but
his body was racked with a fit of
coughing and spluttering, and
he dropped to his knees. He felt

something coiling behind him, some part of him that didn't feel familiar. *My tail.* The thought seemed to come out of nowhere.

What's happening to me...?

Up ahead, not far off, he saw a cave formed out of massive red boulders and, in the cave mouth, a puddle of water shaded from the sun. Tears of relief sprang to his eyes. *A drink, at last!*

He scuttled over on all fours. But as he was about to plunge his face into the water, he gasped.

A hideous reflection was staring back at him. A face of ridged skin

that was hardened and glistening.
Red eyes glowed within hollow
sockets.

His hands flew up to touch the
strange features. But there was
something wrong with his fingers.

They felt stiff, and he couldn't flex them. He looked down and saw that they were hardening too, and darkening in colour, turning a sickly green.

His stomach tensed with fear. *The witch's spell...*

The ground trembled, as though a sleeping giant had stirred somewhere deep below.

"Mackey?"

The voice came from behind him. Mackey lumbered to his feet, turning to face the newcomer.

For a moment, he couldn't believe his eyes. It was a girl on a white horse, with a golden axe slung from the saddle. Then he recognised her.

One of those meddling kids, he realised. *The ones who landed us in the dungeons in the first place.* The girl was small and slight, with a shock of dark hair and a determined look in her eye. But Mackey didn't miss the flicker of horror that crossed her face when she saw him full on.

"You..." he hissed. His voice came out low and hoarse. It didn't sound like his at all.

"My name is Katya." She swung her leg over the saddle and slid to the ground, unslinging her axe and holding it loosely in one hand. "And you need to come with me."

Mackey snorted with anger. If the New Protectors hadn't arrested him, he'd never have met that sorceress in the dungeon. None of this would have happened. He would still be himself. Good old crafty Mackey. Not...whatever he was now.

He took a step back.

"I can help you." Katya approached slowly, like he was a startled horse that needed taming. "Come back to the palace. Daltec can cure you, I promise. Just—"

Mackey let out a howl of fury, his voice rattling strangely. *I'm never going back to that dungeon.* He wanted to say it, but the words wouldn't come.

Instead he threw himself forwards, swiping at the girl. She darted to one side and he fell, exhaustion overtaking him as he slumped to the ground. His knees slammed into the rocks, but he felt no pain. His knees were covered with thick, armoured plates now, just like his face and hands.

"Please..." The girl held her arms

wide, letting the axe dangle on a strap from her wrist. "I won't hurt you."

Rage surged through Mackey like poison. He dived at her again, bearing down on her with all his weight. He was bulky now, and heavier than he'd ever been. He lifted her easily.

Mackey caught one last glimpse of the girl's flailing arms and legs, her eyes wide with shock as he threw her. She disappeared, tumbling down over the edge of the canyon. Her horse let out a neigh of terror. Then it bolted, kicking up dust and loose rock.

Alone again.

The girl was dead, for all Mackey

knew. *But what do I care?*

His breaths were coming hard
and fast. He struck out, blindly
heading off across the rocks. The
heat from beneath the ground
seemed to grow with every step.

But the heat in his belly was fiercer by far. It burned him up like fire until he couldn't think straight.

Who am I? Where am I going?

A sudden burst of pain stabbed through his back. He felt his spine shifting, like it was being bent and twisted it into a new shape.

What's become of me?

He lifted his shaking hands to his face. But they weren't hands any more.

They were now vicious, serrated claws.

Mackey opened his mouth to scream, but a faintness came over him. He sank to the ground.

Then, at last, the darkness clouded everything.

LUCKY

Katya blinked, groaned and screwed up her eyes against the sunlight.

Ouch... She winced as she tried to roll over. Her shoulder hurt. Her head hurt.

Come to think of it, everything hurt.

Twisting her neck, she could see

the lip of the canyon high, high above, a stark line against the bright blue sky. No wonder she wasn't feeling so good. Quite a fall!

Gritting her teeth against the stabs of pain, she hauled herself into a sitting position. Her forehead throbbed. She had stabbed her axe into the cliff-face to slow her fall when she went over the edge. *But I wasn't quick enough*, she thought ruefully, touching her fingertips to her forehead. They came away wet with blood.

She flexed her fingers and shifted her legs. Nothing seemed

to be broken, at least. Her axe was
buried blade-first in the dusty red
ground a short distance away. The
strap must have slipped off her
wrist in the fall.

What have you done, Mackey? She wanted to shout with frustration, but she had a feeling it would hurt too much. If only he understood the danger he was in. If only he wasn't so stubborn and would let her help him. She dreaded to think what might have happened by now.

What he might have become.

A low rumble sounded behind her. At first she thought it was a minor earthquake. They were common enough here, so close to the volcanoes of Tangala.

But no...

She could hear something

moving now. Slow, careful steps. A predator's steps. And suddenly she understood that it hadn't been a rumble at all. It was a growl.

She turned and caught her breath. Prowling across the rocks towards her was a sleek feline creature, almost as big as she was. It had pointed ears, black markings across its sandy fur and sharp teeth bared in a hostile snarl.

A bobcat!

Katya lunged for her axe, but it was out of reach, and her fingers just grasped at sand.

The bobcart darted forwards.

Ignoring the pain, Katya rolled to one side, snatching up the axe as she sprung to her feet. Her head swam as she dropped down into a fighting crouch. "It's all right..." she said, trying to keep her voice steady. "Take it easy."

The bobcat just arched its back and stalked closer. It was probably hungry. Or maybe it had cubs nearby. Katya backed away, looking all around. Her stomach clenched as she saw that there was no way out of the canyon. In fact, it was more like a sinkhole, with sheer sides all around. No cover, either.

Only one thing for it... *I've got to drive it off.*

Katya flipped the axe in her hand so she was holding out the butt instead of the blade. She didn't

want to hurt the animal. But maybe the thick wooden handle would be enough to give it a fright.

She drew herself up, trying to look as big as possible. She stamped the ground. "Yaaah!"

The bobcat paused, one paw raised...then kept coming.

"YAAAH!" Katya dived forwards, swiping the axe handle. "Shoo! Go away!"

The bobcat cringed. Then, lighting fast, it turned and scampered off, its bushy tail from waving side to side. When it reached the canyon wall it launched itself upwards, darting from rock to rock, climbing the wall as easily as Katya climbed stairs.

Katya watched enviously as the bobcat slipped over the top of the canyon and disappeared. *Easy enough for you*, she thought.

Her heart sank at the thought of the climb. She didn't want to fall again... She'd been lucky the first time, but if she survived a second tumble, it would be a miracle.

Her gaze fell on the purple gemstone on her golden ring. *I could use it to summon Tom*. But she felt uneasy at the idea. The Master of the Beasts had still been suffering from

Malvel's poison when she'd last seen him. And besides, what if one of the other New Protectors was in trouble and needed him more?

Heaving a sigh, Katya slung the axe at her hip, wiped the sweat from her hands and headed for the canyon wall. She could remember the route the bobcat had taken. *At least I know those rocks aren't loose.*

The sun beat down as she began to climb. She hauled herself up, the rocks digging into her palms and fingers. Within moments, her tunic stuck to her back and her eyes stung with sweat.

Up close, she saw that the canyon wall wasn't just made up of red rock with a few scrubby bits of yellow grass sprouting here and there. Patches of black crystal could also

be seen in places, glittering despite the dust that covered them. Black diamonds. Katya knew that much of Tangala's wealth was thanks to these gemstones.

Her muscles ached, but she pushed on. Halfway up, her foot slipped and sent rocks skittering down. She clung on, her heart beating wildly.

One foot at a time. I'll get there.

And at last, she was hauling herself up over the canyon edge, gasping with relief. For a moment she lay, gazing up at the sky, feeling lucky to be alive. But she knew there was no time to linger. Katya clambered to her feet and set off, stumbling across the rocks. But her horse was gone, and Mackey was nowhere to be seen.

He can't have got far.

She saw scuff marks in the thin layer of grit that covered the ground. A trail. She followed as best she could. Occasionally she lost the tracks, only to find them again. They were uneven, as if Mackey was stumbling. Sometimes it looked as though he'd even fallen onto all fours. The sorceress Zuba's magic had done something terrible to him.

It's up to me to find out what that is... and put a stop to it!

BLACK DIAMONDS

As her aches and pains faded, Katya strode faster. It was a relief, but she still couldn't see any sign of Mackey. She thought of how strange he had looked: his skin, harder than before, had turned a kind of green, and his back had curved, beginning to hunch... and strangest of all was the grotesque tail that had sprouted behind him.

Katya shuddered and hurried on. The dry, dusty terrain didn't change, but the ground was getting hotter – so hot that she worried her boots would catch melt if she stopped for too long. Clouds of steam rose up here and there, and the earth was cracked.

As she crested a rise, she spotted something on the plateau beyond. It was a cluster of tents, the dusty red canvas almost invisible against the rocks. But she could see movement between them — men, women and children bustling, arguing and playing, all dressed in light tunics. Smoke rose from cooking pots.

Nomads. Katya's heart lifted at the sight. The horse had taken her water flask with it when it bolted, and it was hours since she had drunk anything. Her throat was parched raw.

Perhaps they'll have even caught my horse. Or Mackey...

She broke into a run, half-skidding down a slope as she headed for the little camp.

"Stop!"

Katya stumbled to a halt, heart racing at the sudden cry. Up ahead she saw a small girl with a thick cloud of white hair, standing at the edge of the camp and waving an arm wildly. "Left!" shouted the girl. "Step left, now!" Her eyes were wide, her brow creased with anxiety.

What the...? Katya was about to call back, when she felt the ground burning through her boot's soles all the way to her feet.

"Whoa!" She threw herself left, just as the girl had instructed. There was a rumbling, like the

roar of a buried dragon. Then –
WHOOOSH! – hot water sprayed
up from the ground, right where
Katya had been standing. Steam

belched out in all directions.

Geysers!

Katya crouched, flinging her arms over her head as rocks rained down on all sides, thumping into the ground, thrown free by the force of the geyser.

Nervously, she lowered her arms and looked up.

That was close!

"Here!" yelled the girl, beckoning. "To me!"

This time, Katya didn't think twice. She ran, feet pounding the rocks as she charged across the geyser field until she reached the girl. She stopped, bent over and panting.

"Are you all right?" asked the girl.

Katya nodded and smiled. "You saved my life!" she gasped. "Thank you."

The girl just shrugged and stuck out her hand. "I'm Daffnee," she said. "And you must be very stupid."

Katya's smile faded. "What do you mean?"

"No one goes wandering through the geyser fields," said Daffnee. "No one but us, anyway. It's much too dangerous."

Katya felt herself grinning, in

spite of herself. She could tell that Daffnee wasn't trying to be rude – she was just honest. "I suppose you're right. I'm Katya."

"Pleased to meet you," said Daffnee, as they shook hands. "We can be friends, even if you are stupid."

Katya tried very hard not to laugh. "I don't understand, though," she said. "How did you know the geyser would blow?"

"It's a bit complicated," said Daffnee, looking doubtfully at Katya. "But I'm a Listener. Mum is a Listener too. So was Grandad." She placed a palm flat on the ground. "Mum says it means we're sort of... friends with the land. I understand what it's going to do next. Does that make sense?"

"Sort of," said Katya.

A crowd of the nomads had begun to form around them. They all had the same pale skin and blond-white hair as Daffnee, and they were all peering curiously at Katya. The adults had little black dots tattooed in lines across their cheeks and colourful beads woven into their hair.

"Hello," said Katya, smiling to

show she was friendly. "And why do you live here, if it's so dangerous?"

"Black diamonds, of course," said Daffnee. "They form in the streams that come from the geysers. We don't stay anywhere for too long. We strike camp and move on somewhere else once we've harvested all the diamonds in area. Or if a volcano erupts," she added, with another shrug.

"And who is this?"

A shadow fell over Katya, and she spun round to see that a new group of nomads had just arrived. They were big, strong men and women,

all with dazzling white hair and
dotted tattoos. Their leader, the one
who had spoken, was tall and wiry,
and leant on a long walking staff
topped with a chunk of glittering

black diamond. He wore a pair of strange goggles, leather with transparent black lenses, and his companions all had them too, slung round their necks.

Katya remembered stories she had heard, back in Pania, of how miners wore those special sun-goggles to reflect the sun's rays when they worked.

"This is my new friend, Katya," said Daffnee. "She's not very bright, but I like her anyway."

"I am Ross," said the tall man, pulling off his goggles and nodding to Katya. "I lead this clan. You're very lucky. You could have been killed getting here."

"I would have been if not for Daffnee," said Katya. "But I had no choice. I've been given a Quest by Queen Aroha."

"The Queen?" Ross raised his eyebrows. "Then perhaps we can be of assistance?"

"Have you seen a thin man with a tail, hunched over, with strange green patches on his body?"

The miners all shook their heads. "We would surely have recognised such a person," said Ross.

Katya smiled, but inside she was

feeling glum. Mackey could be miles away by now...

Just then, she caught a glimpse of movement on the ground. She looked down and gasped. Scorpions! Dozens of the dark little creatures scuttled across the rocks, each as big as a hand. Some were even scurrying over the feet of the nomads.

Katya backed away.

"They don't sting, silly," said Daffnee, with a giggle. "Well, not usually."

Ross was frowning though. "So many of them..."

All going in the same direction.

"They're running from something," said Katya. Her mouth felt suddenly dry.

"A geyser, probably," said Daffnee. "They can tell when one's about to blow."

"That's not it." Katya pointed. "They're running towards the geysers."

Sure enough, the scorpions were streaming in a glistening black mass out across the geyser field that Katya had just crossed.

Gasps and cries rose up around. They all turned.

And there on the horizon, heading towards the camp with a strange, shuffling, walk, was something that froze Katya's blood.

It was a monster. A hideous Beast,

half human, and half...something else.

It's Mackey, Katya realised. Or it used to be. His eyes now glowed red. He had grown larger, and the green patches on his skin had bulked into solid armour plates. His tail was segmented and curved stiffly overhead, a stinger glistening green at the end.

He's a giant scorpion!

SHADOW OF THE BEAST

Tom tapped his foot impatiently, watching Daltec. The wizard sat hunched over a massive, dusty old tome laid out on a reading desk. He was frowning as he scanned the yellowed pages. The only light came from a candle beside him, a soft glow that flickered on the spines of a thousand ancient books on shelves all around.

"Any luck?" asked Elenna, stepping into the library. The wizard didn't even look up.

Tom knew there was no hope of getting Daltec's attention when he was so deep in his research. Instead, he tiptoed forwards to peer over his friend's shoulder. The writing was dense and full of strange, arcane language. But he recognised a word repeated here and there throughout the page. Netherworld.

His skin prickled as he thought
of the purple smoke that had
flowed into Rafe's hammer. Could
that strange substance have come
from there? He cast a glance at the

hammer itself, propped up against Daltec's desk. It looked...ordinary.

He felt a gentle tingle in his hand. He looked down he saw the blue jewel of his ring glowing brightly in the darkness.

"One of the New Protectors," said Elenna. "They must be in trouble."

Tom stepped away from Daltec's desk, lifting the ring up to eye level. A ball of deep blue light rose from the ring, slowly forming into the face of Katya. She had a gash across her forehead, and Tom could tell from her frown that something was very wrong.

"I'm sorry, Tom..." muttered Katya. "I didn't want to call on you, but—"

"You need help," said Tom. "Don't worry, I'll be there."

"Are you sure?" asked Elenna, raising an eyebrow.

Tom nodded. He hadn't had a chance to rest yet, and his body was still heavy with weariness. *But while there's blood in my veins, I'll never abandon my friends.*

"I'll come too." It was Rafe who had spoken. Tom and Elenna turned to see him standing in the doorway, his brow set with determination.

"No," said Daltec, looking up from

the book at last. "You mustn't leave this palace. I am still in the process of examining your hammer – you cannot set off on a Quest unarmed. Besides, the magic is not powerful enough for three of you to travel." He looked worried, Tom noticed. *What has he discovered in that book?*

Rafe's shoulders slumped, but he nodded all the same.

Elenna unslung her bow, and Tom adjusted his sword and shield.

"Ready, Elenna?" he asked.

"Ready, Tom."

Tom twisted the ring once. A rumble like thunder sounded

through the library, and Tom felt
the floor shudder beneath his boots.
Yellow light flared in front of them,
blinding bright. Tom blinked.

When he looked again, he saw that
a doorway had formed there, out of
thin air – a rip in reality, with jagged,
glowing golden edges.

Together, he and Elenna stepped
through.

Nausea surged through Tom as
he stumbled out the other side. He
threw up his hands to shield his eyes
from sudden, bright sunlight.

Elenna bent over beside him,
hands on her knees. "Urgh. I don't

think I'll ever get used to that..."

"Tom? You came!"

Tom turned to see Katya hurrying over to him, looking relieved. "Are you all right? You don't look well.

What happened to the others?"

Elenna told Katya about Rafe's victory over Hyrix. Tom took in his surroundings. The ground was hot beneath them. A geyser field. A short way off, he saw a cluster of tents pitched on the field, where pale, white-haired nomads gathered, looking anxiously into the distance.

Tom followed their gaze, and felt his blood run cold.

There, on the horizon, a creature was approaching. A huge, monstrous bulk, much bigger than a man, with massive pincers instead of hands and green armour that gleamed in

the sunshine. It shambled forward
with a strange, loping gait.

Half man, half scorpion.

A Beast.

"Zuba's enchantment..." muttered
Elenna, as she saw it too. "Look what
it's done to Mackey."

"Who are these strangers?" said
a tall nomad, wearing dark-glass
goggles and carrying a staff.

"They've come to protect you," said
Katya. "Tom, Elenna – this is Ross,
the leader of this tribe. And Ross, this
is the great Tom and the amazing
Elenna, legendary heroes of Avantia!"

There was a short silence, as the

nomads cast nervous glances
among each other.

"Are you sure?" said a little girl

with a cloud of white hair.

Tom couldn't help smiling. *We probably don't look our best right now!*

Ross slammed his staff down on the ground. "Guards, to me!"

The tents rustled, and more men and women spilled out. They looked bigger and more muscular than the other nomads, and they carried pick-axes, clubs and mallets. They gathered round Ross.

"Friends!" said Ross, in a deep, booming voice. "You have always protected our camp from thieves, looking to steal our diamonds. Now I ask you to protect something far more valuable — the lives of our people!"

A murmur of agreement rose up from the armed nomads. They began pulling on dark-glass goggles of their own, and tightening their grip on their weapons.

"The rest of you, stay back!" called Ross.

The guards formed a line at the edge of the camp, facing the Beast, while the other nomads moved back behind them, huddling together.

"We'll stand with you," said Tom, taking up a position in the line, with Elenna and Katya at his side.

Ross gave him a doubtful look. "If

you're sure," he said.

Elenna notched an arrow to her bowstring. Tom drew his sword, wrapping his fingers tight around the grip. He unhooked his shield, held it up in front of him and dropped into a fighting stance.

Even after so many Quests, he still felt a shiver of unease at the thought of facing the Beast that was prowling ever closer.

"Tom?" whispered Katya. She was shifting from foot to foot, holding her axe tightly in both hands. "I feel...nervous."

Tom did his best to smile. "That's

good," he told her. "Nerves keep you alert. Just remember – whatever happens, stay calm."

Katya didn't look reassured. But she nodded all the same.

They waited, watching the Beast. He was so close now that they could see his eyes, ghastly red and glowing with an odd, magical light. His armour plates clicked and rattled as he moved. His pincers scissored, snapping at the air, and his tail was plump and segmented, the vicious tip dripping green venom that splashed and sizzled among the rocks.

Tom could almost feel the nomad guards' fear. He heard one gasp, and saw another take a half-step back.

They're going to lose their nerve...

With a deep breath, Tom stepped out of the line. He strode forward, sword and shield raised, until he stood in the shadow of the Beast.

Up close, Tom saw how big the scorpion monster really was — more than twice Tom's height, and heavy with his armour plating. Through the magic of the red jewel of Torgor, Tom heard the Beast's hideous rattling voice.

I am Makoro. I will lay waste to this

land.

"You're not Makoro," said Tom, making his voice as loud and brave as he could manage. "You're just Mackey. I can see it in your face. You don't have to do this, Mackey. You don't have to be a monster. Fight the Beast!"

For a moment, Tom could have sworn he saw something in that twisted face — a twitch of the mouth that made him think of Mackey's lopsided grin. Then it was gone.

I am Makoro. Prepare to meet your doom.

The Beast stepped forwards, getting ready to strike.

Tom struck first, slicing his sword at the Beast's leg. But Makoro's pincer was quick to block the blow. *CLANG!* Tom's sword bounced off the scorpion's armour like it was solid rock.

WHUMP! The second pincer slammed into Tom's shield, knocking him aside. He rolled over and over until he smacked into a boulder and lay there, dazed, the sky spinning above him.

No time to lie around! He leapt back to his feet.

Elenna and Katya were shouting, getting the guards to circle the Beast. One brave nomad lunged and swung a mallet at Makoro's back. The Beast didn't even seem to notice.

Those weapons are useless! Tom realised. *His armour is too tough.*

Another guard leapt forwards, but Makoro just lazily swung his pincer, and the nomad shied away.

Katya let out a war cry and dived in, axe swinging, but the Beast suddenly let fly with a kick. Tom saw Katya crumple to the ground, winded.

The shadow of the Beast fell over her.

"No!"

Roaring with fury, Tom called on the power of his golden leg armour. He felt the magical speed surge through him, filling his legs and powering him forwards. He skidded in between Makoro and Katya, lifting his shield and bracing as the Beast's pincer smashed down. The blow folded him to his knees, and the next moment he saw the glistening green point of Makoro's tail curve overhead, arcing down towards him.

A FALLEN HERO

"No!" Katya gasped as she saw the Beast's pointed stinger whip down...

Fszzshhh! With a hiss, thick goo spurted from the stinger, spattering Tom's shield. Green smoke wafted from it, and a horrendous stench stung Katya's nostrils.

What is that stuff?

Tom grunted, staggering back. Now Katya saw, with dawning horror, green slime dripping from his forehead, his cheeks, his chin. *It's all over his face!*

Katya leapt to her feet. Tom was

stumbling blindly, and the Beast was creeping closer, pincers opening, ready to strike...

"Back, foul creature!"

Turning, Katya saw Ross striding forwards, his staff held out like a spear. Her stomach lurched with alarm. *There's no way he'll hurt the Beast with that thing!*

Then she saw the tip of the staff flash, so blindingly bright she had to look away. The black diamond was catching the sunlight, redirecting it like a mirror. She saw the circle of light cast by the diamond move across the rocks, as Ross angled the staff until it shone right in the Beast's eyes.

The monster let out a horrible, rattling howl. He shambled to a halt, swiping his pincers to block the light. Ross just calmly side-stepped, angling the light from the diamond so that it kept shining in Makoro's face.

With another hiss and a screech of fury, the Beast retreated, scuttling behind a rocky outcrop. He was gone.

"That...was amazing..." breathed Katya. She felt dizzy, her limbs heavy as the adrenaline of the fight seeped away.

Ross didn't even smile. "That thing

will be back soon enough," he said. He lowered his staff and called to his people. "Strike camp! We must leave this place at once." The nomads set about taking down tents and snuffing out cooking fires.

Katya ran over to where Tom had fallen. Elenna was already there, kneeling at his side, her brow knit with worry. Tom had sunk to the ground, head buried in his hands.

"Will you let us take a look?" asked Elenna, gently.

Tom lowered shaking hands. Katya couldn't hold in her gasp of shock.

The green substance clung to his

face and filmed his eyes. "I can't see," he croaked.

"We can fix this," said Elenna, her jaw set. "We just need to get back to the palace. Daltec will know what to do, if we—"

"No!" Tom gripped her forearm hard. "We have a Quest to finish. I've never given up, and I'm not starting now."

Katya didn't know what to say. She couldn't believe Tom's courage. *But he can't defeat the Beast – not like this!*

"He fought bravely." Katya saw that Ross had arrived. He leant on his staff, a grave expression on his face.

"I underestimated you three."

"It was you who drove the Beast away," said Katya. "That diamond..."

"Tangalan black diamond can focus the power of sunlight," said Ross, nodding at the tip of his staff. "Used carefully, it can burn any living creature."

"You saved Tom's life," said Elenna, holding her friend in her arms. "Will you help him a second time? Will you look after him, while Katya and I draw Makoro away from your camp?"

Ross nodded stiffly. He hesitated, then unhooked two pairs of dark-glass goggles from his belt and held them out. "These will protect your eyes from the sun — and from the Beast's poison."

"Thank you." Katya pulled the goggles on. The world turned grey.

A commotion at the camp made them all turn. Then Katya saw little Daffnee scurry out from behind a half-dismantled tent. "It's coming back!" she squealed. "I can feel it in the ground!"

Her eyes were wide with terror, and Katya felt a shiver run down her spine.

So Makoro wasn't escaping... just getting ready to attack again.

Katya spotted a flash of darkness, as

the Beast darted out from behind a cluster of boulders on the far side of the camp. Screams rang through the air.

Makoro had circled around, outflanking the line of guards. And now he was inside the camp.

She saw the Beast dash in among the nomads, venomous tail waving. She saw people running, dragging children after them, cradling babies in their arms as a tent collapsed, its poles snapped clean in two by the Beast's fearsome pincers. Makoro reared up, letting out a triumphant death rattle.

"Wait!" shouted Elenna.

Too late, Katya saw why. Ross was running straight for the Beast.

"These are my people!" the nomad leader roared. "Be gone!"

As he ran, he levelled his staff again.

But this time he had come too close. Makoro struck like lightning, pincers clamping down on the weapon.

CRRACCK! The wood shattered, and the ruined staff dropped to the desert floor.

Ross stumbled to a halt, frozen with shock.

Thump!

Makoro's pincer slammed into
the nomad leader, sending him
sprawling like a rag doll.

1

COME AND GET ME

Katya stared in horror. Ross lay utterly still, not moving a muscle.

Is he alive...?

There was no time to find out. Makoro was rampaging on through the camp. The Beast overturned a cooking pot, stamped on the coals and shredded another tent with a swipe of his tail. The guards had dropped their weapons to save their families. Fear was spreading through the nomads like wildfire.

"You stay with Tom," Katya told Elenna. "Protect him."

"What about you?" asked Elenna.

"I'll handle Makoro." Katya strode forwards, without waiting for a reply. Her palms were slick with sweat, her stomach churning with fear. But she gritted her teeth and tightened her grip on her axe. "You!" she shouted. "Scorpion man! Come and fight me, if you dare!"

Makoro froze. His sickly red eyes turned on Katya, and his jagged mouth clicked and shifted. *Like he's licking his lips...*

Katya took a step back as the Beast approached. *Come on!* She kept on backing up, drawing Makoro away from the camp and on to the rocky geyser field.

Here, out in the open, none of the nomads would be at risk from those deadly pincers.

Katya danced forward, swinging her axe with all her strength. *CLANG!* Her arms juddered painfully as the blade bounced off an armoured plate. She stumbled, off balance.

The axe hadn't even made a scratch. Makoro made a horrible chittering sound. Katya could have sworn he was laughing at her.

Then her heart thundered as the Beast dropped into a crouch, tail raised...

Whhhshhh!

Katya rolled to one side as a gout of green venom spewed from the tail, spattering the ground where she had just been standing. It sizzled and hissed, giving off foul-

smelling smoke. *That was close!*

She stood, her mind racing. Her axe was clearly useless against Makoro. *So how am I supposed to beat him?* She stamped her foot, frustration threatening to overwhelm her.

Stay calm. That was what Tom had told her. She took a deep breath, forcing herself to slow down. Think clearly.

You've never failed a Quest. You've never let your kingdom down.

And you're not going to today.

Makoro was lumbering forwards again, pulling back one huge pincer for a side-swipe. Katya launched herself straight at him, darting under the Beast's limbs and running, leading Makoro further from the camp. She could hear him thundering after her.

"Not that way!"

Throwing a glance over her shoulder, she saw Daffnee. The little girl was bouncing up and down, waving her arms wildly. "Geyser!"

Now Katya noticed that the ground was heating up beneath her. It felt as though it might blow at any moment.

Her heart was pounding as she skidded to a halt, an idea forming in her brain.

A crazy, foolish idea. But it was the only one she had.

The Beast didn't like the burning sunlight. So I bet he won't like scalding hot water either!

"Elenna!" she called, her voice sounding hoarse. "Can you slow him down?"

Makoro was still charging towards Katya. But beyond, she saw Elenna fit an arrow to her bow and let fly.

Thunk! The arrow buried itself in a gap between the Beast's armour plates. Shrieking with fury, Makoro stopped to yank at the shaft with a pincer.

Katya stepped lightly through

the geyser field, feeling the
heat through her boots. It grew
increasingly hot, until she was sure
she was in exactly the right place.

Looking up, she saw Elenna's eyes go wide. *She's guessed what I'm doing...*

"No!" yelled Elenna. "It's too dangerous!"

"Don't be stupid!" screamed Daffnee, clutching desperately at her hair.

Katya shifted from foot to foot. The leather of her boots was smoking now, and she felt sure her feet might catch fire at any moment.

She would only get one chance... and if she timed it wrong, it was all over. Tangala would be doomed.

She adjusted her goggles, making sure they fitted tightly.

The Beast had finally pulled the arrow free and tossed it away. Elenna had another ready, notched on her bowstring. But Katya shook her head.

"Makoro!" she cried, throwing her arms wide. "I'm here! Come and get me!"

NOT FOR A
MOMENT

The earth trembled as Makoro charged.

He bore down on Katya, looming closer and closer. A solid mass of glistening green shell, pincers raised like scythes, poised to rip her to pieces. Every instinct in Katya's body was screaming at her to turn and run away.

But she held her nerve.

She heard the clatter of his jaw, his rattling breaths as he descended on her. And now one great claw was stretching open wide, angled just so, to snap her head from her body...

Now!

She flung herself backwards, rolling and tumbling among the rocks, coming to rest just in time to see—

WHOOOMPH!

Water roared from the ground where she'd stood, a spurt as thick as a tree trunk, boiling, frothing

and hissing as it slammed into Makoro and tossed him upwards.

Katya's heart leapt. Through the veil of volcanic mist, she caught glimpses of the Beast turning in mid-air, thrown up like a child's plaything. Then down he fell, speeding faster and faster until he hit the ground.

THUMP!

The earth shook once again. The surge of water slowed, splattering away to nothing and leaving behind only the lingering hiss and gasp of steam.

Slowly, cautiously, Katya rose to her feet. She approached, axe held ready.

Makoro lay jerking and twitching in a puddle of steaming water. The Beast's tail lashed weakly, and she saw that its stinger was crushed and bent out of shape, seeping green venom that spattered the desert floor.

Suddenly, Makoro swayed to his feet. He looked unsteady, pincers jabbing madly at imaginary foes. He let out a terrible rattling sound, like a grunt of pain. The stinger of his tail was withering like a rotting piece of fruit. The Beast stumbled and flailed.

He's afraid, Katya realised. And

that made her feel braver.

She bounded forward and swung her axe, as hard as she could. The blade sliced through the Beast's tail, as easy as if it were damp wood. The stinger fell with a soft thump among the red rocks.

Makoro screeched again, sinking to his knees. Then, finally, he slumped face-forward, smacking into the ground.

Dust rose from the rocks. A strange silence seemed to descend all around, as though the kingdom was holding its breath.

Katya picked her way across the

rocks, her heart still beating madly in her chest.

When she reached the Beast's head, she lifted her axe high, ready to bring it down.

She hesitated. The yellow light in Makoro's eyes seemed fainter now, almost gone entirely. And there was something else. She could see fear there. He knew he was defeated.

With a soft sighing sound, a purple smoke coiled from the Beast's body. Katya started in alarm, but before she could react, the smoke flowed into her axe. In a moment it was gone.

She lowered her axe, staring in astonishment at the blade.

It looked just the same.

But she sensed that somehow it was different.

What in all Tangala...?

Something else was happening now, she realised. The body of the Beast was shrinking, the armour plates shimmering away in a purple haze of light, until a much smaller, more fragile body was left behind. The body of a tall, skinny man, curled up with his arms held protectively over his head.

Mackey looked up at her, the terror plain in his hollow eyes.

"Please..." he stuttered. "Please... Don't kill me."

He looked exhausted. Deathly pale. And no wonder. Who could

say what it had taken out of him, transforming into a terrible, murderous Beast and back again?

Katya smiled grimly as she slung her axe at her hip. "Like I said before, I'm not going to hurt you," she said. "I'm just going to take you back where you belong – the palace dungeons."

Hearing footsteps, Katya turned to see two of the nomad guards arrive at a run. They grabbed Mackey by his arms and hoisted him to his feet.

"Look after him," said Katya, as the nomads escorted Mackey back

to the camp. "And don't worry. He'll be coming with me when I return to Pania."

"Are you all right?" Other nomads were arriving now, gathering round

Katya in a grateful crowd.

"You saved us!"

"Did the Beast harm you?"

"I'm fine." Katya gently pushed through the throng and made her way to where Tom sat, still slumped on the ground. Her heart leapt to see that Ross was there too, crouching with Elenna next to Tom. He was pale and bleeding from a gash on his arm, but he was alive.

As Katya knelt beside them, Ross was just tying a bandage around Tom's eyes.

"Katya?" said Tom, his voice not much more than a whisper. "Did you defeat the Beast?"

"I did." Relief rushed through her, taking her by surprise, and tears pricked at her eyes. "It's over," she murmured.

Tom's cracked lips curved into a smile. "I never doubted you. Not for a moment."

"But what about you?"

Tom waved a hand dismissively. "This? It's nothing." But Katya could tell from the effort in his voice that it wasn't nothing.

"I can do no more," said Ross, as he finished tying the bandage and sat back. "Alas, I am no healer."

"Daltec will know what to do," said Elenna, her voice full of determination. "I'm sure of it."

But Katya couldn't tell if she really believed her own words.

She looked up to see a little girl standing some way off, with a cloud of white hair.

Daffnee.

The nomad girl smiled, her big eyes wide. "Thank you, Katya," she said quietly. "For saving us." She hesitated a moment. "Maybe you aren't so stupid after all."

Katya snorted. "As long as you're my friend, you can call me what you like."

It felt good to laugh, even for just a moment.

But a moment is all it can be.

The danger wasn't over. Not even close.

Katya gazed out at the jagged peaks of volcanoes on the distant horizon. Somewhere out there were two more Beasts, created by Zuba's evil magic. Beasts that could destroy the whole kingdom if the New Protectors didn't stop them.

Miandra and Nolan, wherever you are... thought Katya. *Don't give up the Quest!*

THE END

CONGRATULATIONS, YOU HAVE COMPLETED THIS QUEST!

At the end of each chapter you were awarded a special gold coin.
The QUEST in this book was worth an amazing 8 coins.

Look at the Beast Quest totem picture opposite to see how far you've come in your journey to become

MASTER OF THE BEASTS.

The more books you read, the more coins you will collect!

Do you want your own
Beast Quest Totem?

1. Cut out and collect the coin below
2. Go to the Beast Quest website
3. Download and print out your totem
4. Add your coin to the totem

www.beastquest.co.uk

READ THE BOOKS, COLLECT THE COINS!
EARN COINS FOR EVERY CHAPTER YOU READ!

550+ COINS
MASTER OF THE BEASTS

550+
515
480
445

410 COINS
HERO →

410
395
380
365
350

350 COINS
← WARRIOR

320
290
260

230 COINS
KNIGHT →

230
217
206
191
180

180 COINS
← SQUIRE

146
112
78

44 COINS
PAGE →

44
30
19
8

8 COINS
← APPRENTICE

SHIFTERS

Don't miss the next exciting Beast Quest book: LEPTIKA THE NOCTURNAL NIGHTMARE!

Read on for a sneak peek...

SORCERERS OF THE PAST

Daltec set down the scroll he was studying and rubbed his aching eyes. His neck was stiff and the light in his tower room was fading fast. He glanced up through the narrow window and saw a thin sliver of moon shining brightly in the deepening blue of the summer sky. Worry clamped around his heart like a fist. *It will be dark soon, and I've found nothing useful!*

Daltec had spent most of the day desperately leafing through ancient texts. That morning, a young sorceress called Zuba had cursed four bandits in Aroha's dungeons, changing them into human-Beast hybrids. The four bandits had escaped and were now wreaking havoc on Tangala. *If I don't work out how to reverse Zuba's enchantments, who knows how many innocent people will die?*

As Daltec lifted another scroll, pushing his dread and weariness aside, his candle flickered and almost went out. He glanced again at the window with a frown. No wind stirred the trees outside and the door to his chamber was shut, but still, the flame wavered. Suddenly, a shaft of light sliced through the air before him, making him squint. The bright beam widened, becoming a shining portal and a dark figure stepped through, silhouetted for an instant against the silver glow. Daltec supressed

a groan as the portal vanished and he made out his tall, fair-haired visitor. Stefan — secretary to the Council of Wizards. Dressed in flowing purple robes, the young man ran his gaze around Daltec's chamber, pursing his lips in distaste.

"So, is this what passes for a

Wizard's quarters in Tangala?" Stefan asked, one slender eyebrow raised. "Quaint." Daltec took a steadying breath. He had chosen his chamber due to its remoteness from Queen Aroha's household, not for its comfort. The tower room was cramped, with his few belongings piled in a corner. He had been due to travel back to Avantia that morning with Elenna and Tom, but his journey home was aborted due to Zuba's evil enchantments. He had not yet fully unpacked.

"I have everything I need," Daltec said, trying to keep the irritation from his voice. "Everything, that is, apart from the assistance I requested. When I contacted the Council, I was hoping they would send a senior Wizard."

Stefan sniffed. "As you might imagine, the Council is very busy preparing for the annual vote for a new Judge. They will only make time for real emergencies. Tell me, why did you take it upon yourself to call at such a time?"

Daltec pinched the bridge of his nose. He could feel a headache coming. Stefan always seemed to have that effect on him. "I can assure you the matter is urgent," Daltec said. "A sorceress has come to Tangala, claiming that she is of the Metamorphia line. She calls herself Zuba and has cast a spell over four bandits, turning them into Beasts. The creatures have rampaged through Pania and beyond. We are doing our best to recapture them, but they have... unnatural powers."

Stefan shrugged. "A few Beasts? That sounds like a regional issue to me — something you should be well equipped to deal with."

Daltec nodded. "Of course. And

normally, I wouldn't involve the
Council of Wizards where Beasts
are concerned. I am more worried
about the sudden appearance of
this sorceress. As you know, the
Metamorphia were believed to
be long gone. I thought I should
inform the Council. My research
has shown that the Metamorphia
weren't always in conflict with
the Council — in fact they used to
create man-Beast hybrids to help
Masters and Mistresses of the
Beasts. But I believe ultimately, the
Metamorphia were cast out."

"That is correct," Stefan said. "But

we have only your word that this woman is a real threat. I will let the Council know of your concerns, of course..." Stefan smiled thinly. "But as I said, they are very busy."

Daltec slapped the palm of his hand down hard on his desk. "Too

busy to investigate the possible return of the most powerful sorcerers ever known?" he demanded.

Stefan frowned, his pale eyes flashing with anger. "I shall see what I can do." He cast a final, scornful glance around the chamber, then swirled his cloak around himself and vanished in a flash of light.

Alone once more in his shadowy chamber, Daltec closed his eyes and breathed deeply to get his temper under control. So, no help from the Council then... It had been unwise to snap at Stefan, but the man was less use than a paper sword. Daltec picked up another scroll, ready to continue his research, when a young servant boy with a flushed face burst into the room.

"Sir!" the boy said. "Elenna and Tom have returned. Tom needs your attention urgently. The Beast, Makoro, sprayed him with some kind of poison!" Daltec leapt up and hurried from the room. "They are in the infirmary!" the servant called after him.

Daltec reached the long, dimly lit ward to find Tom sitting on the edge of a bed with his back to the door. A nurse was dipping a long bandage in a basin of steaming water that smelled of pine. Elenna stood beside Tom, her brows pinched together with worry. Hearing Daltec enter, she turned. "Is there anything you can do?" she asked. "We've already tried Epos's healing talon, but the enchantment's too strong."

Daltec crossed to the nurse's side. "I'll leave this with you," she said, handing Daltec the warm bandage. Daltec turned his attention to Tom. A thick film covered his eyes,

obscuring the pupils, and the skin
of his lids looked angry and red.

"Let me see," Daltec said, gently
lifting Tom's chin. Tom winced
slightly but didn't draw back. Daltec
picked up a lamp and held it close
to Tom's staring eyes, looking for

any reaction. Tom didn't even blink. "Is Makoro still on the loose?" Daltec asked, trying to keep the worry from his voice.

"No," Elenna said. "He's transformed back into the bandit Mackey now, and he's in the dungeon along with Hyrold. But that still leaves two of Zuba's creations on the loose. Nolan and Miandra are searching for them."

"I should be out there with them," Tom said as Daltec wrapped the bandage carefully around his head. "How quickly can you restore my sight?"

Daltec paused. He knew of many salves and poultices, but none of them would work quickly – if at all.

"There are several healing spells I can try," he said at last. "But they will take time, and you'll need to rest."

Tom shook his head fiercely and started to rise. "I need to be out there now!" he cried.

Read
LEPTIKA THE NOCTURNAL NIGHTMARE
to find out what happens next!

Battle galactic monsters alongside heroes Harry and Ava in Space Wars

FROM THE CREATOR OF BeastQuest
ADAM BLADE
SPACE WARS
MONSTER FROM THE VOID

FROM THE CREATOR OF BeastQuest
ADAM BLADE
SPACE WARS
COSMIC SPIDER ATTACK

FROM THE CREATOR OF BeastQuest
ADAM BLADE
SPACE WARS
DROID DOG STRIKE

READY FOR YOUR NEXT QUEST?

VISIT

WWW.BEASTQUEST.CO.UK

FOR MORE...